Ian Beck's
LOST
on the
BEACH

SCHOLASTIC
PRESS

For Lily

Teddy Bears have such a quiet life,
don't they?

Scholastic Children's Books,
Commonwealth House, 1-19 New Oxford Street,
London WC1A 1NU, UK
a division of Scholastic Ltd
London ~ New York ~ Toronto ~ Sydney ~ Auckland
Mexico City ~ New Delhi ~ Hong Kong

Published by Scholastic Ltd, 2002

Text and illustrations copyright © Ian Beck, 2002

ISBN: 0 439 97905 6

Printed in Dubai.   All rights reserved

2 4 6 8 10 9 7 5 3 1

Ian Beck has asserted his moral right to be identified as the author and illustrator of this work
in accordance with the Copyright, Designs and Patents Act, 1988.

It was a hot afternoon on the beach. Lily was busy playing in the sand. Teddy was just sitting.

"I like your sandcastle," said Mum, when Lily
finished digging.
"It's a house for Teddy," said Lily.

Mum laid out a towel and set Teddy down.
"Come on," she said, "let's leave Teddy here
while we go for an ice-cream."

"Wait," said Lily, and she tied a handkerchief
around Teddy's head.
"That'll keep you cool while I'm gone," she said.

Teddy sat quietly in the hot sun. But then, whoops! He fell backwards as something tugged at his towel.

A small puppy had a corner of Teddy's towel in his teeth.

As the playful pup began to pull . . .

. . . Teddy bump, bump, bumped across the beach.

When the puppy
let go, Teddy was
over by the rocks,
and a long, long
way from his
sandcastle home.

For a while he clambered happily about.
In between the rocks were pools of seawater
with all kinds of creatures in them.

He had fun splashing his paws in the water
until – ouch! – he was pinched by a crab.

Then he sat down for a rest. And suddenly he felt his bottom getting wet. Oh dear, the tide was coming in!

He could see the sandcastle house on the other side of the beach. But how could he get back across the water? He was trapped!

Teddy spotted some seagulls flying overhead.
Quickly he took off his handkerchief.
"Yoo-hoo!" he waved.

A friendly gull flew down and picked him up.

Wheeeee! Teddy was lifted high into the sky.

Whoosh! He was flying through white fluffy clouds.

Then whoops! Teddy let go – and he was falling, down, down, down until . . .

. . . he grabbed the
corners of his
handkerchief to
make a parachute!

Slowly he drifted
down and landed
on a piece of wood
floating on the waves.
Phew!

Teddy bobbed up and down in the water for
a while. But soon he began to feel cold.
The beach seemed a long way away now.

"I MUST get back to Lily," he said. He could just see the little red flag on the sandcastle house, and he began to paddle towards it.

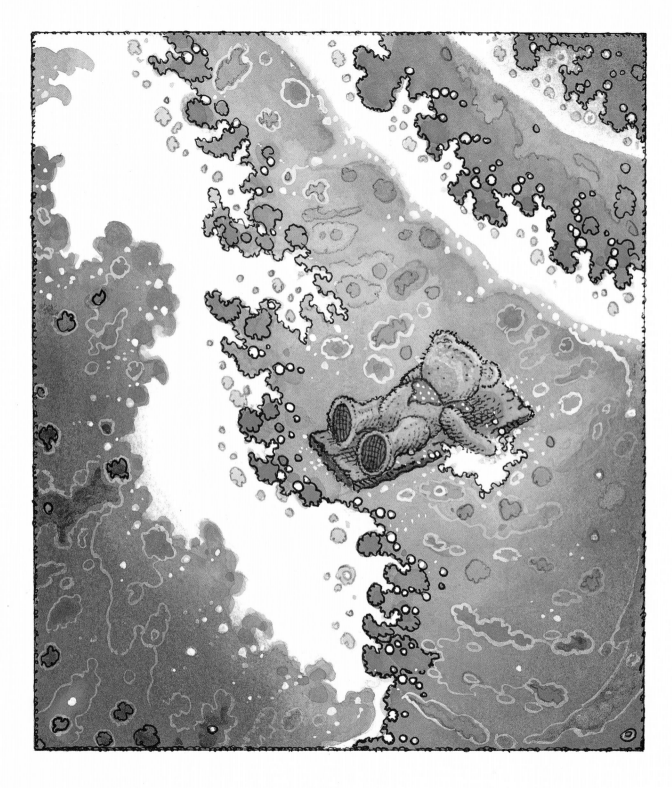

Suddenly he heard a roaring sound. A HUGE wave was coming up behind him!

The wave lifted him right out of the water,
higher, higher and higher still, until . . .

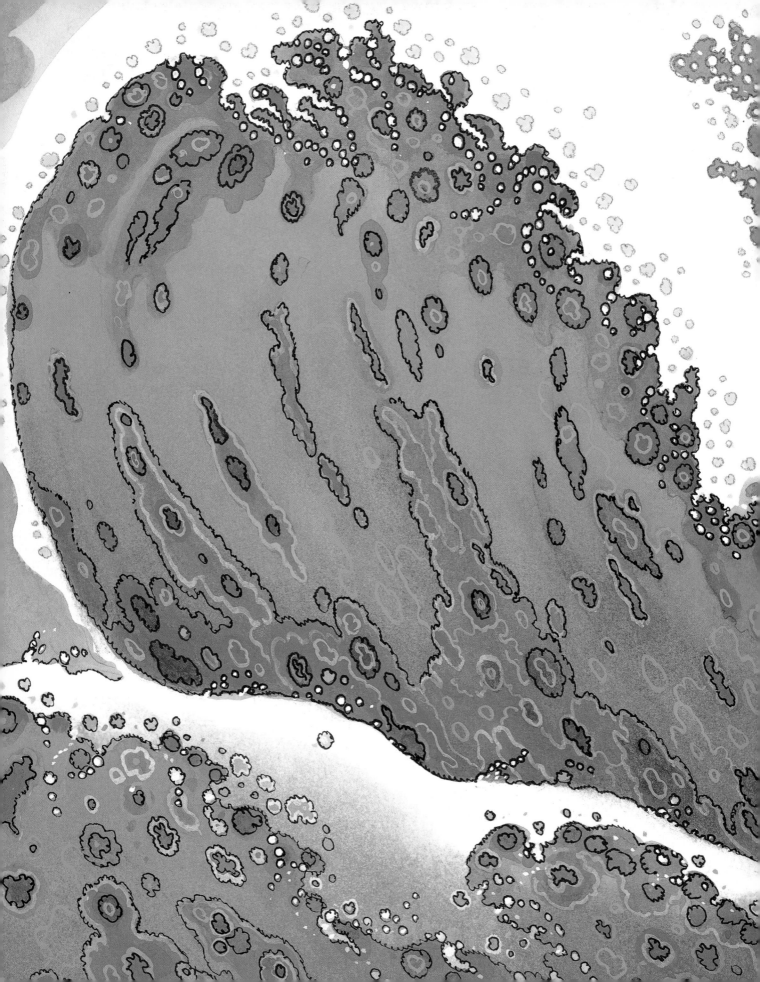

Wheeeee . . . eee,
he was surfing!
What fun!

With a crash the wave dumped Teddy – plomp! – on to the sand. He was back on the beach, where he had started.

It was hard work crossing the beach because
his paws kept sinking in the soft sand . . .

. . . but at last he was back at his sandcastle home. He put his handkerchief on his head, sat down and waited.

When Lily came back she gave him a cuddle.
"Oh Teddy," she said, "why are you all wet?
You don't have much luck, do you!"

Good Night, Lily. Kiss kiss.
And Good Night, Teddy. Sleep tight.
But we know what really happened, don't we?